GRANDMA'S BUTTON BOX

by Linda Williams Aber
Illustrated by Page Eastburn O'Rourke

The Kane Press
New York

Book Design/Art Direction: Roberta Pressel

Library of Congress Cataloging-in-Publication Data

Aber, Linda Williams.
    Grandma's button box/Linda Williams Aber; illustrated by Page Eastburn O'Rourke.
    p.   cm. — (Math matters.)
    Summary: When she spills her grandmother's button box, Kelly and her cousins try to sort them by size, color, and shape and they earn Grandma's gratitude.
    ISBN 1-57565-110-6 (pbk. : alk. paper)
    [1. Set theory—Fiction. 2. Buttons—Fiction.] I. O'Rourke, Page Eastburn, ill.
    II. Title. III. Series.

    PZ7.A1613 Gr 2002
    [E]—dc21   2001038805
                                                                                          CIP
                                                                                           AC

10 9 8 7 6 5 4 3 2 1

First published in the United States of America in 2002 by The Kane Press.
Printed in Hong Kong.

Kelly and her cousins were visiting Grandma. One morning Kelly woke up to a very quiet house. Her three cousins were asleep. Grandma was taking a walk.

Kelly ate breakfast by herself and wondered what to do.

"What can I do that won't wake everyone up?" she thought. "Television's too loud. Piano's too loud. Even shooting baskets is too loud."

Then, while Kelly was getting dressed, she heard a tiny *ping*! A button had popped off her shirt.

"That's it!" she thought. "Grandma's button box!"

Grandma had the coolest buttons! Even the plain ones seemed special, because Grandma told stories about them.

There were pearl buttons from Grandma's wedding dress and train buttons from Kelly's baby sweater. There was a soft furry button and a fancy gold one with big jewels on it.

lost for 3 years
turned up in doghouse

snapped off
Grandpa's Groundhog
Day suspenders

Kelly hadn't played with the button box all summer. "It's the perfect quiet thing to do!" she thought.

The button box was on a high shelf next to Grandma's sewing table. Kelly had to stand on a stool to reach it.

She reached up as high as she could.

Grandma's button box wobbled. The top snapped open. Buttons flew everywhere. CRASH! The box hit the floor.

Timmy and Brendan came running
down the hall.

"What happened?" asked Brendan. Then
he saw the buttons. "Uh-oh," he said.

"You're in trouble now," said Timmy.

"You guys have to help me," said Kelly. "I'll never find all the buttons by myself."

"Sure," said Brendan.

"If you take me bowling," said Timmy.

"Deal," said Kelly.

Everyone started searching.

"Look! Here's one
in the flowerpot,"
said Brendan.

"Here's one in
Grandma's slipper!"
shouted Timmy.

Kelly crawled into the closet.
"There's a bunch of them in here!"
she yelled.

"Wow!" said Timmy. "I found six
under the rug."

Soon all the buttons were in a big pile.

"What a mess!" said Timmy. "I'll put them back in the box."

"Wait!" said Kelly. "We have to put them back in the right compartments."

"How did Grandma have them sorted?"
asked Brendan. "By size? Shape? Color?"

"I can't remember," said Kelly.

"Uh-oh," said Brendan.

"You're in BIG trouble now!" said Timmy.

"Maybe they were sorted by shape," said Kelly.

"Let's try it," said Brendan.

Timmy picked out all the round buttons.

Brendan found some square ones and a few that were shaped like triangles and diamonds.

Kelly started to pick out everything else. She found star shapes, ducks, boats, and cowboy boots. There was an umbrella, two apples, an elephant, and a pineapple.

"How do I sort these?" she asked.

"You've got me," said Brendan.

"How about sorting them by size?" said Kelly.

"You mean we have to do it *again*?" said Timmy.

After a while they had seven piles of buttons.

"Let's see," said Kelly. "We've got teeny, small, medium, large, extra-large, jumbo, and humongous."

Kelly sighed. "This isn't right, either."
"There are twelve compartments," said
Brendan, "and only seven sizes."
"I GIVE UP!" yelled Timmy.

19

"What's all the shouting about?" asked Sara, Kelly's oldest cousin.

"Kelly spilled Grandma's buttons, and now they're all mixed up," Timmy said.

"We tried sorting them by shape," said Kelly.

"But that didn't work," said Timmy.

"We tried sorting them by size," said Brendan.

"And that didn't work either," said Timmy.

Sara looked at the buttons. "There must be another way," she said. "What about…"

"Sorting them by color!" said Kelly.

"Exactly," Sara said.

Sara and Kelly picked out the buttons that were white, pink, purple, yellow, orange, and brown.

Brendan and Timmy picked out the buttons that were red, blue, green, silver, gold, and black.

"We've got twelve colors," said Kelly.

"A color for every compartment!" Brendan said. "Perfect."

"Finally," said Timmy.

"Hi, kids!" called Grandma a few minutes later. "I'm home!"

"We're in the sewing room," called Sara.

"Oh, my goodness!" said Grandma. "You sorted my buttons!"

"Kelly spilled them," Timmy said. "But we found them all."

"We put them back by color," said Kelly. "That's the way you had them, isn't it?"

"No," said Grandma. "It isn't."
"You're in GIGANTIC trouble now,"
Timmy said to Kelly.

27

Grandma laughed. "I never sorted them, honey bunny," she told Kelly. "They were always just jumbled together." "All that trouble for nothing?" said Timmy.

"It wasn't for nothing," said Grandma. She took off her sweater. "See these safety pins? I never bothered to look for new buttons because it always took so long to find anything in that button box."

"Let's look for some new buttons now," Kelly said. "It won't take long at all."

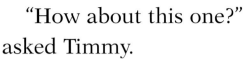
"How about this one?"
asked Timmy.

"Wrong color," said
Brendan. "I like this one."

"Wrong size," said
Kelly. "How about
these? They're almost
perfect."

Kelly was right. The buttons looked great on Grandma's sweater. "I think I'll keep my buttons sorted from now on," she said.
And she did.

SORTING CHART

You can **sort** these buttons in different ways.

Sort them by **shape**.

All round!

Sort them by **color**.

All Yellow!

Sort them by **size**.

All large!

Can you think of another way to sort them?
(Hint: Check the holes.)